A Bill Martin Book
Henry Holt and Company　　　New York

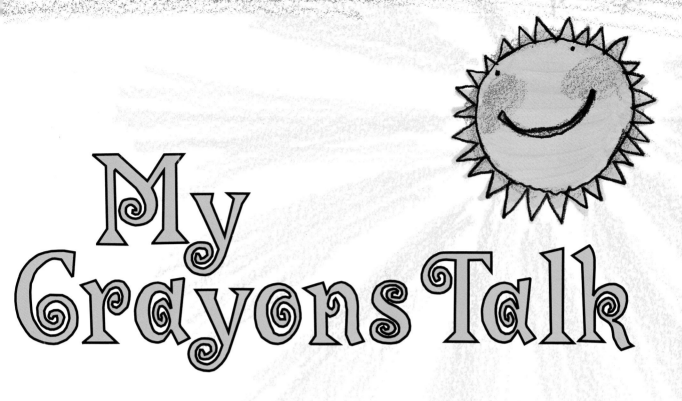

My Crayons Talk

PATRICIA HUBBARD

illustrations by

G. BRIAN KARAS

Talk. Talk.
My crayons talk.
Yackity. Clackity.
Talk. Talk. Talk.

Purple shouts, "Yum!
Bubble gum."

Brown sings, "Play,
Mud-pie day."

Blue calls, "Sky,
Swing so high."

Yellow chirps, "Quick,
Baby chick."

Talk. Talk.
My crayons talk.
Yackity. Clackity.
Talk. Talk. Talk.

Gold brags, "Fine,
Dress up time."

Silver toots, "Grand,
Marching band."

Red roars, "No,
Do not go."

Green yells, "Fun!
Watch me run."

Talk. Talk.
My crayons talk.
Yackity. Clackity.
Talk. Talk. Talk.

Orange asks, "Sweet,
May I eat?"

Black hoots, "Wise,
Big owl eyes."

White screams, "Most
Scary ghost."

Pink laughs, "Clown!
Pants fall down!"

Talk. Talk.
My crayons talk.
Yack yack yackity.
Chit chat clackity.
Yackity. Clackity.
Talk. Talk. Talk.

Bill Martin Jr, Ph.D., has devoted his life to the education of young children. Bill
Martin Books reflect his philosophy: that children's imaginations are opened up
through the play of language, the imagery of illustration, and the permanent joy of
reading books.

Henry Holt and Company, LLC, *Publishers since 1866*
115 West 18th Street, New York, New York 10011
www.henryholt.com

Henry Holt is a registered trademark of Henry Holt and Company, LLC

Library of Congress Cataloging-in-Publication Data
Hubbard, Patricia.

My crayons talk / by Patricia Hubbard; illustrations by G. Brian Karas
"A Bill Martin Book"
Summary: Brown crayon sings "Play, Mud-pie day," and Blue crayon calls
"Sky, Swing so high" in this story about talking crayons. [1. Color—Fiction.
2. Crayons—Fiction. 3. Stories in rhyme.] I. Karas, G. Brian, ill. II. Title.
PZ8.3.H8475My 1995 [E]—dc20 95-12786

ISBN 0-8050-3529-X (hardcover)
15 14 13 12 11 10 9 8 7 6
ISBN 0-8050-6150-9 (paperback)
15 14 13 12 11 10 9 8 7 6 5

First published in hardcover in 1996 by Henry Holt and Company
First Owlet paperback edition—1999
Printed in the United States of America on acid-free paper. ∞

The artist used crayons, gouache, acrylic, and pencil on Strathmore bristol board
to create the illustrations for this book.